D0099572

Evan's Corner

Story by
Elizabeth Starr Hill

Pictures by
Sandra Speidel

Puffin Books

PUFFIN BOOKS
Published by the Penguin Group
Penguin Books USA Inc., 375 Hudson Street, New York, New York 10014, U.S.A.
Penguin Books Ltd, 27 Wrights Lane, London W8 5TZ, England
Penguin Books Australia Ltd, Ringwood, Victoria, Australia
Penguin Books Canada Ltd, 10 Alcorn Avenue, Toronto, Ontario, Canada M4V 3B2
Penguin Books (N.Z.) Ltd, 182–190 Wairau Road, Auckland 10, New Zealand

Penguin Books Ltd, Registered Offices: Harmondsworth, MIddlesex, England

First published in the United States of America by Holt, Rinehart and Winston, 1967
Slightly revised edition with illustrations by Sandra Speidel published by Viking Penguin,
a division of Penguin Books USA Inc. 1991
Published in Puffin Books, 1993

10 9 8 7

Text copyright © Elizabeth Starr Hill, 1967, 1991
Illustrations copyright © Sandra Speidel, 1991
All rights reserved

LIBRARY OF CONGRESS CATALOGING-IN-PUBLICATION DATA
Hill, Elizabeth Starr.
    Evan's corner / by Elizabeth Starr Hill; illustrated by Sandra
Speidel.   p.   cm.
    "First published in the United States of America by Holt, Rinehart
and Winston, 1967; published in 1990 with new illustrations by
Viking Penguin, a division of Penguin Books USA Inc."
—T.p. verso.
    Summary: Needing a place to call his own, Evan is thrilled when
his mother points out that their crowded apartment has eight
corners, one for each family member.
    ISBN 0-14-054406-2
    [1. Family life—Fiction.   2. Apartment houses—Fiction.   3. Afro-
Americans—Fiction.]   I. Speidel, Sandra, ill.   II. Title.
[PZ7.H5514Ev 1993   [E]—dc20   92-25334

Printed in the United States of America
Set in Caledonia

Except in the United States of America, this book is sold subject
to the condition that it shall not, by way of trade or otherwise,
be lent, re-sold, hired out, or otherwise circulated without the
publisher's prior consent in any form of binding or cover other than
that in which it is published and without a similar condition including
this condition being imposed on the subsequent purchaser.

Since Evan's Corner *was first published, many thousands of children have shared Evan's story with me. This new edition of the book is dedicated to all young readers who, like Evan, long for a place of their own.*

E. S. H

To Isiah Redd and his mom

S.S.

Evan walked home from school slowly. He stopped in front of a pet shop. In the window, a canary sang to him from its golden cage.

Canary bird has its own cage, Evan thought. I *want a place of my own.*

He walked on. A bright pink flower on a windowsill caught his eye. *Flower has its own pot*, he thought. *Wish* I *had a place of my own.*

At the big crossing, he waited by the newsstand for the light to change. *Paper man has his own stand*, he thought. *And I — I need a place of my own.*

He crossed the noisy, busy street and turned into the building where he lived. He trudged up four flights of steep stairs to the two rooms he and his family shared.

Soon his three sisters and two brothers would come home. Then his mother and then his father. *Mighty lot of family*, Evan thought. *And no place to call just* mine.

Evan wore a door key on a string around his neck. But today the door flew open before he touched it.

"Surprise!" His mother stood laughing in the doorway. "Mrs. Thompson said I could leave early! I beat you home, Evan!" Mrs. Thompson was the lady his mother cleaned for.

Evan gave his mother a big hug. He burst out, "Mama, you know what I've been wishing for *hard?*"

"Tell me." His mother smiled.

Evan told her the canary bird had a cage. He told her the flower had a pot. He told her the paper man had a newsstand. He ended, "And *I* want a place of my own."

His mother thought and thought. Then her face lighted up. "Why, of course!" she said. "It will work out just right. There are eight of us. That means each of us can have a corner!"

Evan jumped to his feet and clapped his hands. "Can I choose mine?"

"Yes." She nodded. "Go ahead. You have first choice, Evan."

Evan ran to every corner of the rooms. One had a pretty edge of rug. Another had an interesting crack in the wall. But the one Evan liked best, the one he wanted for his own, had a nice small window and a bit of polished floor.

"This is mine," Evan said happily. "This is my corner."

Evan's mother shared the kitchen down the hall with another lady. Often Evan kept her company while she fixed supper. But that night he paid no attention to the rest of the family. He sat alone and content on the floor, in his corner.

His little brother Adam asked him, "Why you want a corner of your own, Evan?"

Evan thought for a minute. "I want a chance to be lonely."

Adam tiptoed away and left him.

When supper was ready, Evan's father came to Evan's corner. "Stew's on the table," he said. "You hungry, Evan?"

"Please, Pa," Evan asked, "if I bring my plate here, can I eat by myself?"

"Why, sure," his father said.

So Evan fetched his plate of stew and sat in his corner again. He

could hear his family talking and laughing. At dessert time, he joined them.

"Why, Evan!" His father smiled. "I thought you wanted to eat by yourself."

Evan smiled back at him. "I was lonely," he said.

After supper, Evan helped clear the table. He brushed his teeth. He studied for school. When his work was done, he went to his corner and looked out the window.

The sky was almost dark. Two pigeons cooed sleepily on the window ledge. Stars lighted up. The breeze blew cooler.

Adam asked softly, "Are you being lonely now, Evan?"

"No," Evan answered.

"What *are* you doing then?"

"I'm wasting time," Evan told him. "In my own way. In my own corner."

Adam asked, "Can I ever come into your corner, Evan?"

"Why don't you choose a corner of your own?" Evan said.

Adam chose the corner across the room from Evan's. He sat in it. He called, "What shall I do in my corner, Evan?"

"Whatever you like."

But Adam didn't know what to do. After a minute, he left his corner. He played horse with his big sister, Lucy. "Giddyap Lucy-horse!" he shouted. They galloped around the room.

Evan watched the pigeons fall asleep on the ledge. He watched the sky get darker and the stars get brighter. Finally, his father called him. "Come out of your corner, sleepyhead! It's time for bed!"

Next morning, as soon as he woke up, Evan ran to his corner. His bit of polished floor shone as brightly as ever. His window was still fun to look through. But Evan felt he needed something more. What could it be?

He stared at the bare walls. *I know!* he thought suddenly. *I need me a picture! And I'll make it myself!*

In school that morning, Evan painted a picture of the sea. He drew big waves and a green boat. He told his teacher, "I'm going to hang this picture in my own corner!"

"That will be lovely, Evan," his teacher said.

Evan could hardly wait to get home after school. He ran past the pet shop. "Canary bird!" he shouted over his shoulder. "I got a place of my own now!"

A-skip and a-gallop, he passed the windowsill with the flower. "Listen, old pink flower," he told it, "I got a place of my own!"

He skidded to a stop at the corner and told the paper man, "Guess what, mister! I'm going to hang this picture in a place that's *just mine!*"

And he skipped and rushed and almost flew the rest of the way.

He taped the picture to the wall beside the window in his corner. He stepped back to look at it.

The green boat seemed to bob on the green waves. It bobbed too much. Evan realized the picture was crooked. He straightened it. Now it looked just right.

Adam came home with their biggest sister, Gloria. She always picked Adam up at the day-care center on her way home.

"That's mighty pretty, Evan!" Adam said. "Do you think I could draw a picture for my corner?"

"Sure you could."

Adam ran off. But he could not find any paper. He had no crayons. Lucy had some, but she was busy with homework now. He returned to Evan.

Evan sat in his corner with his back to the room. He looked up at his picture.

Adam asked softly, "Are you being lonely, Evan? Are you wasting time in your own way?"

"No."

"Well, then, what are you doing?"

"Enjoying peace and quiet," Evan said.

Adam tiptoed off.

That night, Evan lay in bed thinking about his corner. It had a nice floor and a nice window and a nice picture. But was that enough?

No, he decided finally. *I need something more.*

He remembered the pink flower in its pot. He thought: *That's it! I need a plant of my own, in my own corner.*

On Saturday, Evan went to the playground. He took his toothbrush glass and a spoon.

The paving of the playground was cracked. Grass and weeds grew up through the broken concrete. Evan found a weed with big, lacy flowers. He dug it up with his spoon. He planted it in his toothbrush glass.

Then he took it home and put it on the windowsill, in his own corner.

"What you doing, Evan?" Adam asked.

"Watching my plant grow," Evan told him.

"Maybe I'll have a plant, too, someday," Adam said softly.

Evan didn't answer. Something was bothering him. Even now, his corner seemed not quite perfect. And he didn't know why.

I got me no furniture,
he realized at last.
Why didn't I think of
that before?

Evan skipped off to the grocery store. He asked Mr. Meehan for two old orange crates. "Going to make me some furniture," he told Mr. Meehan proudly. "To put in a place of my own."

In his corner, Evan stood one of the crates on end. Now it was like a high desk. He turned the other crate upside down to make a bench. He sat on the bench.

Surely he had all anyone could wish for. And yet . . .

How come I feel like something's still missing? Evan wondered. He puzzled and puzzled over it. Suddenly he remembered the canary bird in its cage.

I know! I need a pet to take care of. A pet of my own, in my own corner. And he ran out to the pet shop.

He looked at the canary bird in the window. *Well, canary bird,* he thought, *you sing fine. But you're not the pet for me.*

He walked into the store. A goldfish swam over to the edge of its bowl and stared at him. Evan thought, *No, sir. That's not the pet for me.*

He moved on to the turtle tank. A sign above it read: BARGAIN! SPECIAL! TURTLE WITH BOWL, ONLY 50¢!

Evan peered into the tank. Several lively turtles swam and scrambled all over each other. One climbed up on a rock in the middle of the water. It looked at Evan.

He felt like laughing. It must have been the funniest turtle in the world! That big old turtle had the *scrawniest* neck. Its feet were wide and ugly. Its eyes were merry. If a turtle could smile, that turtle was smiling.

It took a dive off the rock. Clumsy turtle! It landed upside down in the shallow water! Its legs waved wildly in the air.

Evan turned it over carefully. The turtle winked at him as though it knew a secret.

"Yes, sir, yes, sir!" Evan told that funny old turtle joyfully. "*You're* the pet for me!"

Evan's heart beat hard and fast. He asked the pet-shop man, "Please, mister, do you have a job a boy can do? I'd mighty much like to earn enough to buy a turtle!"

"Sorry, son, I don't need help," the pet-shop man said.

Evan marched from store to store, asking for work. He had no luck.

Maybe some lady would pay me to carry her packages, Evan thought. He turned in at the supermarket. He stood by the checkout counter.

A woman came through. Evan smiled extra-politely. "Excuse me, but those bags look real heavy. Carry them for you?"

"Why, yes." She put them in his arms. "That would be nice."

Evan carried the groceries up the block to where she lived. The woman thanked him. She gave him a dime.

A dime! Now all he needed was four more!

Evan raced back to the supermarket. He stood by the checkout. He waited. Lots of people went past. But none of them wanted him to carry their bags.

Just as Evan began to fear he would never make another cent, a girl said, "Oh, good! I hate lugging bundles!" She, too, gave Evan a dime.

Only three more to go, he thought happily.

On Sunday, the supermarket was closed. But Evan went there right after school on Monday. He made a dime, then another. He had forty cents.

Listen, you old turtle, he thought. *You're almost mine!*

But the next day, he fooled around after school. When he finally got to the supermarket, a bigger boy was there ahead of him.

The day after that, he rushed from school to the supermarket as fast as his legs would go. The other boy was not there.

Hurray! Evan thought. *Bet this is my lucky day.*

At first, things were slow. Then, toward closing time, a white-haired lady spoke to him: "Sonny, do you think you could help me with these heavy groceries?"

Evan said eagerly, "Yes, *ma'am!*"

Her bag was a huge one, filled clear up to the top. Somehow Evan got his arms around it and hoisted it off the counter. "Where to, lady?" he gasped.

"Why," she said sweetly, "I live just next door." She added, "Three flights up."

Evan staggered out of the store with the bag. He thought he never *would* get up those stairs. Yet at last he made it.

"Thank you," the woman said. And she gave him the dime—the wonderful dime—the shining dime that made five!

Evan ran to the pet shop at top speed. He poured the dimes on the counter and said proudly, "I earned some money, mister! I'd like to buy me a turtle!"

The pet-shop man counted the dimes. "All right, son. Choose one," he said.

Evan looked into the tank. His eyes passed from one shell to another. Suddenly he saw a scrawny neck stretch up from the water. A turtle rose, climbed the rock—and fell off upside down, on his back.

"This one!" Evan picked the turtle up. "This one is mine."

Evan carried the turtle home in a bowl. He set it on top of the upturned orange crate.

Adam was already home from the day-care center. He asked excitedly, "What you got now, Evan?"

"My own pet," Evan boasted. "To take care of, in my own corner."

"Evan, do you think I could ever have a pet?" Adam asked.

"Sure. When you're much, much older."

Adam wandered sadly away.

Now Evan had a place of his own. He could be lonely there. He could waste time if he liked. He could enjoy peace and quiet. He had a fine picture to look at. He had a bench of his own to sit on, by his own window. His plant thrived and grew tall. Best of all, he had a pet to love and take care of.

Evan spent most of his spare time in his corner. But he just wasn't happy.

I must need something more, Evan thought. *But what?*

He asked his sisters. They didn't know. He asked his brothers. They didn't know.

His father wasn't home yet. When his mother came home, Evan said, "Mama, I'm not happy in my corner. What do I need now?"

Together, Evan and his mother stood off from the corner and looked at it.

Sunlight poured through the window and gleamed on the floor. The lacy white flowers stirred in the breeze. The turtle seemed to grin through the glass of its bowl. The painted boat rode a painted wave.

Evan's corner was beautiful. They both saw that.

"Evan," his mother said finally. "Maybe what you need is to leave your corner for a while." She smiled into his eyes. "Maybe you need to step out now, and help somebody else."

She left him. He sat alone on his bench, thinking it over.

Adam came in. "Are you enjoying peace and quiet, Evan?" he asked.

"No," Evan said.

"What *are* you doing, then?"

Evan said slowly, "I'm planning to borrow Lucy's crayons."

"Why?"

"To help you draw a picture, if you want to. I'm going to help you fix up your corner. I'm going to help you make it the best—the nicest—the very most beautiful corner in the whole world!"

Joy spread over Adam's face—and over Evan's.

They ran across the room together to work on Adam's corner.